The Huron

CHRISTINE WEBSTER

Weigl

CALGARY

www.weigl.com

Published by Weigl Educational Publishers Limited
6325 10 Street SE
Calgary, Alberta, Canada
T2H 2Z9

Website: www.weigl.com
Copyright ©2009 Weigl Educational Publishers Limited

Library and Archives Canada Cataloguing in Publication data available upon request.
Fax (403) 233-7769 for the attention of the Publishing Records department.

ISBN 978-1-55388-424-8 (hard cover)
ISBN 978-1-55388-425-5 (soft cover)

Printed in the United States of America
1 2 3 4 5 6 7 8 9 0 12 11 10 09 08

Project Coordinator Heather Kissock **Design** Janine Vangool **Layout** Terry Paulhus
Validator Sheila Staats, GoodMinds.com

Photograph credits
Every reasonable effort has been made to trace ownership and to obtain permission to reprint copyright material. The publishers would be pleased to have any errors or omissions brought to their attention so that they may be corrected in subsequent printings.

Cover: Canadian Museum of Civilization (III-H-457, D2004-22577 - main), Alamy (top left), Getty Images (top centre), Alamy (top right); **Alamy:** pages 1, 3, 5, 6, 7, 8, 17, 21, 22; **All Canada Photos:** page 16; **Canadian Heritage Gallery:** page 9 (www.canadianheritage.ca ID #20636, National Archives of Canada C1041); **Canada Museum of Civilization:** pages 10T (III-H-480, D2005-21223), 10M (III-H-453, D2005-11741), 10B (III-H-409 a,b, D2004-23820), 11 (III-H-358, D2002-007814), 14T (III-H-347, D2002-007782), 14L (III-H-318, D2002-008223), 14R (III-H-351, D2002-008339), 15 (III-H-402 a-b, D2002-007780), 20 (III-H-40, D2005-12952), 24T (III-H-62, D2002-007720), 24M (III-H-53, D2002-008301), 24B (III-H-64, D2002-007752), 25B (III-H-464, D2002-007752), 28T (III-H-457, D2004-22577), 28L (III-H-214, D2005-12923), 28R (III-H-99, D2002-007700), 30 (III-H-356, D2002-008469); **Christine Wawanoloath:** page 27; **Getty Images:** pages 12, 13, 18, 19, 23, 26, 29; **McCord Museum:** page 25T.

We acknowledge the financial support of the Government of Canada through the Book Publishing Industry Development Program (BPIDP) for our publishing activities.

Please note
All of the Internet URLs given in the book were valid at the time of publication. However, due to the dynamic nature of the Internet, some addresses may have changed, or sites may have ceased to exist since publication. While the author and publisher regret any inconvenience this may cause readers, no responsibility for any such changes can be accepted by either the author or the publisher.

CONTENTS

The People

The Huron are one of Canada's **First Nations**. They are made up of four groups that merged to form the Huron **Confederacy**, also known as the Wendat. *Wendat* means "dwellers of the peninsula." This is because the Huron lived in the southern part of present-day Ontario. *Wendat* is the word the Huron use to identify themselves. The French gave them the name "Huron" because of the **Mohawk** hairstyles that the warriors wore. The hairstyles reminded the French of the bristles on a wild boar's neck. The term for "boar's head" in French is *hure*.

Huron Map

This map shows the traditional lands of the Huron in Canada.

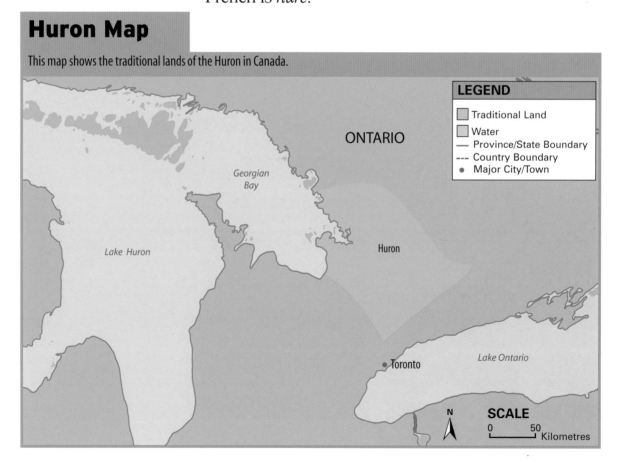

LEGEND
- Traditional Land
- Water
- — Province/State Boundary
- --- Country Boundary
- • Major City/Town

ONTARIO

Georgian Bay

Lake Huron

Huron

Toronto

Lake Ontario

SCALE

0   50
Kilometres

The Huron's traditional lands are found in eastern Canada. The Huron lived in central Ontario, in the areas around Lake Simcoe and Georgian Bay. Some Huron also were found in the St. Lawrence Valley, near what is now the Ontario-Quebec border.

In the 17th century, there were about 10,000 to 30,000 Huron living in the area. Over time, these numbers were greatly reduced by diseases brought by Europeans and conflicts with other First Nations. As their numbers decreased, some of the remaining Huron moved east, while others settled in the United States. Some joined other First Nations. Today, there are about 3,000 Huron. In Canada, most live in a village called Lorette, near Quebec City. In the United States, most Huron live in the states of Michigan, Kansas, and Oklahoma.

Today, most Canadian Huron live on a **reserve** located in Lorette, just north of Quebec City. Here, the Huron have their own government and their own laws. One of the main goals of the Huron government is to keep traditional way of life alive. This is done through organizations such as the Ti-yarihuten Cultural Centre. The centre is responsible for storing and cataloguing **artifacts** from the past, planning traditional activities and events, and promoting Huron artists.

In the 17th century, the French set up missions, such as Sainte-Marie Among the Hurons. The French living at these missions taught the Huron about their religious beliefs.

Huron Homes

In the past, the Huron lived in villages built near water and forests. Water provided transportation routes, allowing the Huron speedy travel to trading partners and hunting grounds. Forests provided lumber for fires and building supplies. Good soil also was important in choosing a location. The Huron relied on soil to grow food crops.

Huron villages were protected by defensive walls. The walls were made up of 9-metre poles that surrounded the village. Saplings were woven between the poles to fill holes and strengthen the walls. Watchtowers also were put up around the village.

Within each village were several longhouses where the Huron lived. Longhouses were about 25 to 30 metres long and had both a width and height of about 6 to 9 metres. Up to six families, including parents, children, grandparents, aunts, and uncles, lived inside.

The Huron used elm, white birch, or alder trees to build their longhouses.

THE MAKING OF A HOME

Longhouses were made from white birch or alder trees. These trees were small and flexible, allowing them to be bent into position easily. Ropes made from braided strips of bark held the bent wood in place. This formed the house's frame. The frame was then covered with elm bark to protect the house from rain and snow. Openings were left in the roof of the longhouse. These allowed smoke to escape. Longhouses had no windows, so the openings also let in sunlight to brighten the home. Doors were placed at each end of the longhouse.

Even though two families shared one firepit, each family was responsible for cooking its own food.

Each house was organized around a main area that contained several firepits. Two families would share one firepit. The firepits were used for warmth, cooking, and conversation. The Huron slept around the firepits on animal skins or mats made of reeds or bark. Other furnishings inside the longhouse included pottery, baskets, and containers of stored corn.

Huron Communities

Everyone in a traditional Huron village had a role to play. Women were responsible for everyday life within the village. They cared for the children, made clothing and baskets, and cooked food. Women also helped obtain food by making fishing nets, gathering berries, and farming the land.

Men protected their villages. They also hunted and fished for food, using tools that they made themselves. Trading was the men's responsibility. They would meet with Europeans and other First Nations to exchange items they needed for items the other group wanted. Everyone in the Huron village shared their food and trade items with each other.

Sometimes, animal skins were combed before being made into clothing.

In the past, Huron children did not go to school. They learned skills by watching and imitating their parents and other adults, as well as by playing games. From an early age, girls were encouraged to help women with the cooking and farming. The boys learned hunting and fishing skills by helping the men.

Huron parents showed tolerance and humour when they raised their children.

The Huron's traditional form of government was based on the **clan** system. Huron clans were matrilineal. This meant that each clan originated from one common female **ancestor**. There were eight Huron clans—Turtle, Wolf, Bear, Beaver, Deer, Hawk, Porcupine, and Snake. Each of these clans were normally represented in every village.

Women known as clan mothers were responsible for selecting a chief. Clan leaders made up a village council or government. They would meet to discuss problems in the village. They would also discuss how to improve day to day life.

Huron Clothing

In the past, everything the Huron ate, built, or wore came from the land. Their clothing was made from the hides and furs of the animals the men hunted, such as deer and beaver. The amount of clothing the Huron wore depended on the season.

During the hot temperatures of the summer months, the Huron wore few clothes. For most of the summer, the men wore only a loincloth, a strip of hide hung from the waist. Women would wear a skirt made from hide. Leather moccasins provided protection for the feet.

In the winter, both men and women protected their legs from the cold by wearing leggings made from hide. Fur cloaks were used as coats. Babies were wrapped in furs as well. As they grew, they were clothed similar to their parents.

Fans cooled the Huron in hot weather. They could be made from animal fur or other materials.

Some Huron clothing had designs embroidered onto it. Before Europeans arrived with thread, moosehair was used to create the patterns.

The Huron added accessories to their clothing. Porcupine quills, beads, and feathers were used as decoration. Often, the Huron wore body paint. Women would use combs made from animal bones to decorate their hair and to hold it back when they were working.

Wampum necklaces and belts were popular as decoration. They were made of polished shells and beads that were strung together. The wampum design recorded an important event.

Wampum belts were normally the width of seven beads. They ranged in length from 0.5 to 2 metres.

Making a wampum belt required great skill. First, the Huron would draw the design that they wanted on the belt on a piece of deer skin. Then, they would prepare the shells for sewing. To turn a shell into a bead, the shell would be rubbed on sandstone until it was cylindrical in shape. A hole was then drilled into the shell by tapping it with a flint-tipped reed.

To make the belt, the beads were sewn onto the deer skin, following the desired pattern. Plant fibre was used as thread. A curved stick worked as a needle.

The Huron used a variety of materials to make headdresses, including velvet, hide, pheasant feathers, and moosehair.

Huron Food

Farming provided most of the food in a Huron village. Corn, beans, pumpkins, and squash were the Huron's main crops. The crops were planted on mounds of dirt that would protect the seeds from frost.

Corn was one of the Huron's most useful crops. Kernels were ground into flour to make a type of cornmeal that could be mixed into soup or baked into bread. Cornmeal could be stored for a long time. It was often used to feed the Huron in the winter months.

Meat was a staple in the Huron diet. Men hunted animals such as deer, bear, beaver, muskrat, and wolf. They also caught fish in nearby rivers or lakes.

The Huron lived in an area that had fertile soil. Many different food plants, including corn, pumpkins, and sunflowers, could be grown successfully here.

RECITE

Honey-Apple Chicken

Ingredients

250 millilitres evaporated milk

2 beaten eggs

160 mL breadcrumbs

30 mL light brown sugar

125 mL raisins

4 chicken cutlets

honey

cooking oil

stuffing mix

3 apples, cored, peeled, and diced

Equipment

Mixing bowl	Frying pan
Small pot	Oven
Tablespoon	Casserole dish

Directions

1. Mix flour, eggs, and breadcrumbs together to create breading. With an adult's help, heat cooking oil in frying pan.

2. Dip chicken cutlets into milk and then in the breading mixture. Fry in pan until golden.

3. Cook stuffing mix and apples in small pot.

4. Place large spoonful of stuffing in centre of cutlet. Roll and press cutlet together, and place in casserole dish.

5. Drizzle honey over cutlets. Cover, and bake at 175 degrees Celsius for 20 minutes. Remove cover, and bake for 5 more minutes.

Tools and Weapons

In the past, the Huron made tools from items they found in their environment. Wood, stone, and bones were all used to make different types of tools. Knives were made by chipping at stone until it had a sharp edge. Other stone tools, such as adzes and pestles, were made by grinding two stones together to shape them. The Huron used adzes for carving. Pestles were used to grind and pound corn to a fine texture.

The Huron used bone to make tools such as awls. An awl is a very sharp tool that works like a sewing needle. The Huron used awls to sew hides together.

Wood was used in combination with stone and bone to make both tools and weapons. Fishing poles and spears were tools that the Huron used to catch fish. Spears were used, along with bows and arrows, for hunting and battle.

Harpoons made from bone were used to catch fish.

Wood and bone were used to make utensils such as spoons, as well as tools such as mauls, or hammers.

HUNTING AND TRAVELLING

Hunting was a part of everyday life for the Huron. Besides bows and arrows, spears, and knives, the Huron used traps to catch animals. The type of trap used depended on the size of the animal. Snare traps, made from tree branches, were used to catch small animals, such as rabbits. Box traps, made from logs, were used to capture large animals, such as bears.

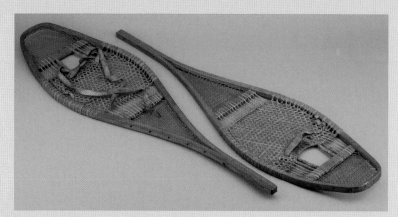

Huron snowshoes were made to travel across open plains. Their long tails helped keep the wearer stable when walking on the snowy surface.

The Huron lived in an area with many lakes and rivers for fishing. They used weirs and spears to trap fish, such as pike, bass, pickerel, and sturgeon. A weir is a fence that is built across a small body of water. When the fish swam into the fenced area, they became trapped, and the Huron were able to spear them.

The Huron used canoes to travel the area's lakes and rivers. Each birchbark canoe was big and sturdy enough to carry four to five men, as well as about 91 kilograms of cargo. The canoes were about 7 metres long and 1 metre wide in the centre.

During the winter months, the Huron used snowshoes to travel the land. Snowshoes were made of wood and strips of animal hide that were tied to the bottom of the wearer's feet. The paddle-like shape of the snowshoes kept the wearer from sinking into the deep snow. Toboggans and sleighs also were used for travelling in the winter.

Huron Religion

Traditionally, the Huron believed in the existence of three worlds. There was a world that contained the dead and spirits, a world of dreams, and the world in which the Huron lived their daily lives. All of these worlds were linked together, with each one having a direct effect on the other two.

The Huron found deep spiritual meaning in the sky, land, and water that surrounded them.

The Huron believed that all living things and objects had a spirit. The most powerful spirit was the sky spirit, who appeared to the Huron as the wind. The sky spirit controlled the seasons and all weather. The land spirit took the form of rocks. It controlled the soil, trees, and other plant life. The Huron believed that the events that took place in their everyday lives were caused by the actions of the spirits.

To the Huron, dreams held special meaning. In some cases, they were omens of events to come. In others, they were believed to express a dreamer's inner and unknown need. If the person did not have this need fulfilled, there was a danger that he or she could become ill. Shamans interpreted the meaning behind the dreams and provided the dreamer with what he or she needed to live a healthy life.

Most shamans were men. They would have visions and dreams that advised on how to solve the mysteries or cure illnesses. Sometimes, a shaman would fast until the solution or cure came to him. Shamans often used herbal remedies and shells when responding to a situation. They were very respected in the Huron community.

Shamans sometimes wore masks while performing healing ceremonies.

The Huron believed that, in the beginning, there was only water and water animals. Then, a divine woman fell from the sky. Two loons broke her fall and held her up with their wings. They cried for help. Together, the animals decided the woman needed ground to live on. Toad went into the water and brought up dirt. This was the start of Earth.

Later, the woman gave birth to twin boys. One was good, and one was evil. The woman died giving birth to the evil twin.

Each boy lived on a different part of Earth. The evil twin made fierce animals like giant toad, who drank all of Earth's water. The good twin created useful animals, such as partridges. The good brother went to the evil brother's land. He found the toad and killed it, and released all of Earth's water.

The two boys had a huge fight. The good twin beat the evil twin, who decided to leave the area and move far to the West. Today, the Hurons believe that, when they die, their spirits go to the West.

Ceremonies and Celebrations

The Huron held many festivals throughout the year. Most of these festivals followed the cycle of the seasons. In autumn, for example, festivals were held to give thanks for a bountiful harvest. To announce a festival or feast, a person walked around the village calling out the details. The older the person making the announcement, the more important the festival was.

The first festival to be held each year was the Maple Festival. It celebrated the arrival of spring by observing the sap that began to run from the maple trees. The Huron gathered to dance, play games, make maple syrup, and feast.

Maple trees begin to bud, or bloom, in late winter or early spring.

The Planting Festival took place in April or May. It was held to celebrate the beginning of a new farming year, when people starting clearing the land and planting their crops. During this festival, the Huron feasted and prayed for good growing conditions for their crops.

The summer months brought the Strawberry Festival and the Green Corn Festival. Both celebrated the ripening of these plants. Speeches, prayers, dances, and games were held to thank the spirits for the bounty these foods brought.

When strawberries were ripe, the Huron knew it was time to plant beans, pumpkins, and corn.

ONONHAROIA

Every winter, the Huron held a winter festival called *Ononharoia*. Unlike the seasonal festivals held throughout the rest of the year, the Ononharoia was more spiritual in nature. It was held as part of a soul cleansing **ritual**. The goal was to chase away all of the evil spirits that brought disease and illness to the village. In order to do this, people who were ill or suffering had to obtain specific objects that had appeared in their dreams. If they were able to find the objects, they would become healthy again. Those who did not find the objects remained ill.

Music and Dance

Both dancing and music played important roles in Huron life. Music often was played during rituals, festivals, or celebrations. Drums made with wood and hide were the main instruments used. The Huron had great respect for the drum. They believed that the beat of the drum echoed the beating of their hearts. Noisemakers or rattles were also used to make music. Sometimes made from turtle shells, these objects would make noise when they were shaken.

Huron songs had special purposes, and were performed on certain occasions. There were songs for specific feasts, to help heal the sick, and to serve as protection against danger. Sometimes, a song would only contain three words. The words were repeated in a rhythmic pattern. Huron women would sing and dance, while the men kept time to the music by tapping on a piece of bark.

Animal horns were often used as rattles. Pebbles or shells would be put inside the horns to make noise.

CEREMONIAL DANCING

Dancing was an important part of traditional Huron life. Some dances were performed only at special ceremonies. Social occasions, such as festivals, also had specific dances that were performed as part of the celebration. Dances, such as the Welcome Dance and the Friendship Dance, were performed throughout the year to begin or end a gathering.

The Blanket Dance was performed to celebrate the election of a chief.

One of the best-known Huron dances is the Great Feather Dance. It is a **sacred** dance that is performed at all Huron ceremonies. The dance is dedicated to a Huron spirit who represents peace. It is danced so that people can reflect on the role of peace in their lives. Both men and women perform the Great Feather Dance. The men form an outer ring, and the women dance inside the ring.

Language and Storytelling

The Huron language is part of the Iroquoian language group. This means that it shares many features with the languages of the **Iroquois** Nations that lived nearby. Due to the decline of the Huron population, the Huron language is in great danger of being lost forever. Today, there is only one person, a college professor from Quebec City, who can speak the language fluently. The Huron are working with him to save the language and pass it on to younger generations. This will help keep the language alive.

Huron reserves in Quebec have both French and Huron languages on their street signs.

In the past, storytelling was an important form of communication for the Huron. While stories were often told in an entertaining way, their main purpose was to teach. Some Huron stories, such as the creation story, present how their world came to be. There are also stories that teach **moral** lessons, explaining how a person's behavior can affect his or her life.

Many Huron stories explain events that occur in nature, such as rainbows.

RAINBOW'S PUNISHMENT

One day, Deer tells Rainbow that he wants to visit his sister in the sky. He asks Rainbow to build him a beautiful bridge to get him there. When Rainbow builds the bridge, however, Deer goes up to the sky and decides not to return. Soon, Bear follows and also decides to stay.

This alarms the other animals, and a council meeting is called. Rainbow is asked to explain why she built the bridge to the sky. She says it is because Deer wanted it.

The council decides that Rainbow must be punished for the disappearance of Deer and Bear. The council burns her bridge to the sky. From that day forward, Rainbow only appears as an arc in the rays of the Sun after a rain shower. She can no longer reach to the sky.

Huron Art

The Huron were skilled artists. Their art included pottery, woven baskets, and quillwork. Most of these items were originally created out of need and were not considered art. European settlers arrived and noted how different the designs and materials were from what they used. The Huron began to trade and sell their handiwork to the Europeans, creating a **cottage industry** for themselves.

The Huron were skilled at making pottery from clay. Clay was pounded and shaped, and then placed in a kiln, or oven, to set. Huron pots had large rounded bottoms that tapered at the top. Designs were etched around the tops of the pots for decoration. Pottery was used as cups and bowls as well as for cooking and storing food.

With the arrival of Europeans, baskets became more decorative. Some were used as ornaments.

Before Europeans arrived, Huron baskets were made to hold and carry various items.

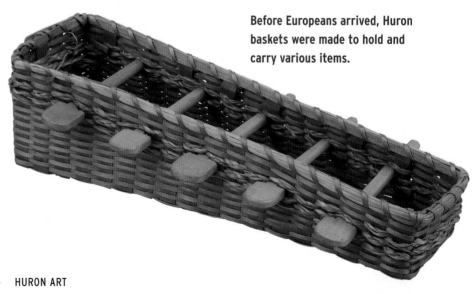

Patterns were embroidered onto birchbark containers, as well as animal hides.

MOOSEHAIR EMBROIDERY

When the Huron settled in the area around Lorette, Quebec, they found many moose. The Huron hunted moose for food and clothing. They used part of the animal to create decorative **embroidery**. The hair on a moose's hump and neck flap is soft but durable. Instead of porcupine quills, the Huron began using moosehair to decorate their clothing. Moosehair patterns often had a floral **motif** and were found on clothing and birchbark containers.

Baskets and mats were a staple in most Huron households. Mats were used for sleeping and sitting. They were normally woven from reeds or cornhusks. Baskets were used to carry or store things. These, too, could be woven using reeds, grass, or cornhusks. However, not all baskets were woven. Some, especially those made from birchbark, were sewn into shape using hide as thread.

The Huron used porcupine quills to decorate their clothing and other items. Working with quills requires much patience as it takes time to plan and create the patterns. First, the quills were pounded until they were flat. Then, they were dyed into many colours. Finally, each quill was woven onto a hide. Depending on the size of the pattern, this process could take days to complete.

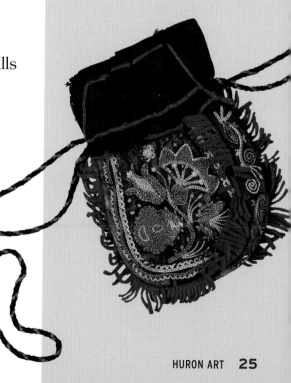

Snow Snake

While much of the Huron's traditional daily life centred around meeting survival needs, there was also time for fun and games. Snow snake was played by the Huron and other First Nations of the Ontario and Quebec woodlands. This was a game the Huron played in the winter, after the men returned from a hunt.

A snow snake is a piece of wood that ranges from 1 to 2 metres in length and is about 2 centimetres in diameter. The goal of the game is to see who can slide their "snake" the farthest down a track. The track is made by dragging a log through the snow to form a gully, which helps the snake stay on course. Some snow snakes can slide more than 1 kilometre under the right conditions.

To play snow snake, people were divided into teams. Each person had a chance to slide the snake, and the distance of each throw was added to a team's score. When everyone had taken their turn, the distances were tallied into a final score. The team that had the highest score won the game.

A snow snake stick is made out of birch or some other hard wood.

Christine Sioui Wawanoloath

Christine Sioui Wawanoloath was born in Wendake, a Huron reserve near Quebec City, in 1952. Her father was Huron, and her mother was Abenaki. After high school, Christine attended Manitou College, a First Nations school in northern Quebec. She developed her artistic skills by studying both art and history. Since leaving Manitou College, Christine has experimented with various types of art, including illustrations, sculpting, and writing. She is best-known for her paintings, which have been displayed in galleries across Canada.

Christine's art is vibrant, humourous, and shows a love for life. Often, the humour is used to delve more deeply into spiritual thoughts and expressions.

Christine delights in creating art that celebrates the importance of living life to the fullest. Her paintings fill entire **canvasses** with bright colours and large images. Christine often uses acrylic paint as her medium. Acrylics are known for their vibrant shades, and they reflect the joy she finds in the world around her.

Today, Christine continues to create her art in Quebec. She also works as the communications coordinator for Terres en Vues/Land InSights, an organization that promotes the art and traditions of Aboriginal Peoples in Quebec and throughout North America.

Christine's art often portrays traditional Huron stories and characters.

Studying the Past

Archaeologists study the past by finding ancient sites where people have lived and examining the artifacts left behind. These artifacts allow archaeologists to piece together the day-to-day occurrences of these people. For example, artifacts made of clay show that this was an important building tool. Weapons made of stone illustrate how ancient peoples hunted.

In Canada, archaeologists have found large pits that the Huron used to bury the dead. They have helped archaeologists learn more about Huron burial traditions. Many artifacts, including necklaces, trinkets, and pottery, have been found in these pits as well. Archaeologists have been able to learn what materials the Huron used to make these items. They have also learned more about Huron pottery. Finding artifacts is an important part of piecing together the past.

Artifacts, such as bowls, toboggans, and embroidery samples, help archaeologists understand how the Huron lived in the past.

TIMELINE

Pre-European Contact

The Huron live in longhouses in villages protected by walls. They leave the villages to hunt deer, bear, and wolves, as well as to fish in nearby lakes and rivers. The Huron farm the land, planting corn, beans, and sunflowers.

1534

Jacques Cartier begins exploring the area in and around the St. Lawrence River, where he first encounters the Huron.

1535

There are 30,000 to 45,000 Huron living in what is now the Ottawa River Valley.

Early 1600s

The French, under Samuel de Champlain, begin to establish trading posts and settlements along the St. Lawrence River.

1614

The Huron agree to a formal trading **alliance** with the French.

1615

French **missionaries** come to live with the Huron. They teach the Huron their religion.

1649-1660

The Huron battle the Iroquois. The Iroquois capture several Huron villages. Some Huron escape and flee to settlements in Quebec, while others move south to the United States.

1666

The French convince the Iroquois to stop fighting.

1693

The Huron begin setting up villages on the outskirts of Quebec City. They finally settle in the village of Jeune Lorette, where most Huron still live today.

Jacques Cartier was one of North America's first explorers. He encountered many Aboriginal Peoples on his journeys.

Make a Clay Pot

The Huron made pottery for use in their everyday life. They collected clay and shaped it into various types of dishes, including bowls and pots. Decorations, in the form of etched patterns, were often added to their creations. Follow the instructions below to make a clay pot similar to those the Huron made.

Materials	• Self drying modeling clay, such as Plasticine	• A sharp wooden stick

Steps

1. Work the clay in your hands until it is soft and flexible.
2. Mould the clay into a bowl shape.
3. Using the stick, etch a pattern into your bowl. Be careful not to squish the bowl, or it will lose its shape.
4. Place your bowl somewhere safe to dry.
5. Once dry, the bowl is complete. Use the bowl as decoration to hold your favourite beads, pennies, or a plant.

Further Reading

Read *Huron-Wendat: Heritage of the Circle* by Georges E. Sioui (University of British Columbia Press, 2000) to explore the history and traditional beliefs of the Huron.

The Huron language and what it represented in Huron society is explained in John L. Steckly's *Words of the Huron* (Wilfrid Laurier University Press, 2007).

Websites

To learn more about how the Huron are preserving their traditional way of life, visit
www.wendake.ca

To read more about Huron craftwork, go to
www.mccord-museum.qc.ca/en/keys/ webtours/CW_HuronWendat_EN.

A detailed history of the Huron is provided at
www.tolatsga.org/hur.html.

GLOSSARY

alliance: a union formed by agreement

ancestor: a relative who lived a long time ago

archaeologists: scientists who study objects from the past to learn about people who lived long ago

artifacts: items, such as tools, made by humans

canvasses: pieces of strong cloth used for painting

clan: a group of people joined together by common relatives

confederacy: a group of people joined together for a special purpose

cottage industry: a business based on selling products that are made at home

embroidery: patterns made on cloth using a thread and a needle

First Nations: members of Canada's Aboriginal community who are not Inuit or Métis

Iroquois: First Nations that live in eastern Canada and the United States; made up of six nations

missionaries: people who teach others about religion

Mohawk: a type of hairstyle based on Mohawk peoples of the past; a strip of hair is left on the centre of the head from the neck to the forehead, and the sides are shaved

moral: having to do with right and wrong

motif: a design theme

reserve: land set aside by the government for First Nations

ritual: a system or form of ceremony

sacred: worthy of religious worship

INDEX